Dear Parent:
Your child's love of reading starts here!

Every child learns to read in a different way and at his or her own speed. You can help your young reader improve and become more confident by encouraging his or her own interests and abilities. You can also guide your child's spiritual development by reading stories with biblical values and Bible stories, like I Can Read! books published by Zonderkidz. From books your child reads with you to the first books he or she reads alone, there are I Can Read! books for every stage of reading:

 SHARED READING
Basic language, word repetition, and whimsical illustrations, ideal for sharing with your emergent reader.

 BEGINNING READING
Short sentences, familiar words, and simple concepts for children eager to read on their own.

 READING WITH HELP
Engaging stories, longer sentences, and language play for developing readers.

 READING ALONE
Complex plots, challenging vocabulary, and high-interest topics for the independent reader.

 ADVANCED READING
Short paragraphs, chapters, and exciting themes for the perfect bridge to chapter books.

I Can Read! books have introduced children to the joy of reading since 1957. Featuring award-winning authors and illustrators and a fabulous cast of beloved characters, I Can Read! books set the standard for beginning readers.

A lifetime of discovery begins with the magical words **"I Can Read!"**

Visit www.icanread.com for information on enriching your child's reading experience.
Visit www.zonderkidz.com for more Zonderkidz I Can Read! titles.

"Each of you must respect
your mother and father"

—*Leviticus 19:3*

ZONDERKIDZ

The Berenstain Bears™ Honey Hunt Helpers
Copyright © 2012 by Berenstain Publishing, Inc.
Illustrations © 2012 by Berenstain Publishing, Inc.

Requests for information should be addressed to:
Zonderkidz, *Grand Rapids, Michigan 49530*

Library of Congress Cataloging-in-Publication Data

Berenstain, Jan, 1923–
        The Berenstain Bears honey hunt helpers / by Jan and Mike Berenstain.
            p.   cm. – (I can read)
        Summary: The Good Deed Scouts help Papa Bear in his attempt to win the prize for
        best honey.
        ISBN 978-0310-72101-7 (softcover)
        [1. Scouting (Youth activity)—Fiction. 2. Honey—Fiction. 3. Bears—Fiction. 4. Christian
    life—Fiction.] I. Berenstain, Mike, 1951- . II. Title.
        PZ7. B44826Bip 2012
        [E]—dc22   2010053520

Editor: Mary Hassinger
Art direction & design: Cindy Davis

Printed in China

12 13 14 15 16 /DSC/ 10 9 8 7 6 5 4 3 2 1

ZONDERkidz

I Can Read!™

BEGINNING READING 1

The Berenstain Bears
Honey Hunt Helpers

Story and Pictures By
Jan and Mike Berenstain

Living Lights™

GOOD DEED SCOUTS

ZONDERVAN.com/
AUTHORTRACKER
follow your favorite authors

The Good Deed Scouts—Brother, Sister,
Fred, and Lizzy—saw a sign:
"Honey contest today.
Big prize for the best honey."

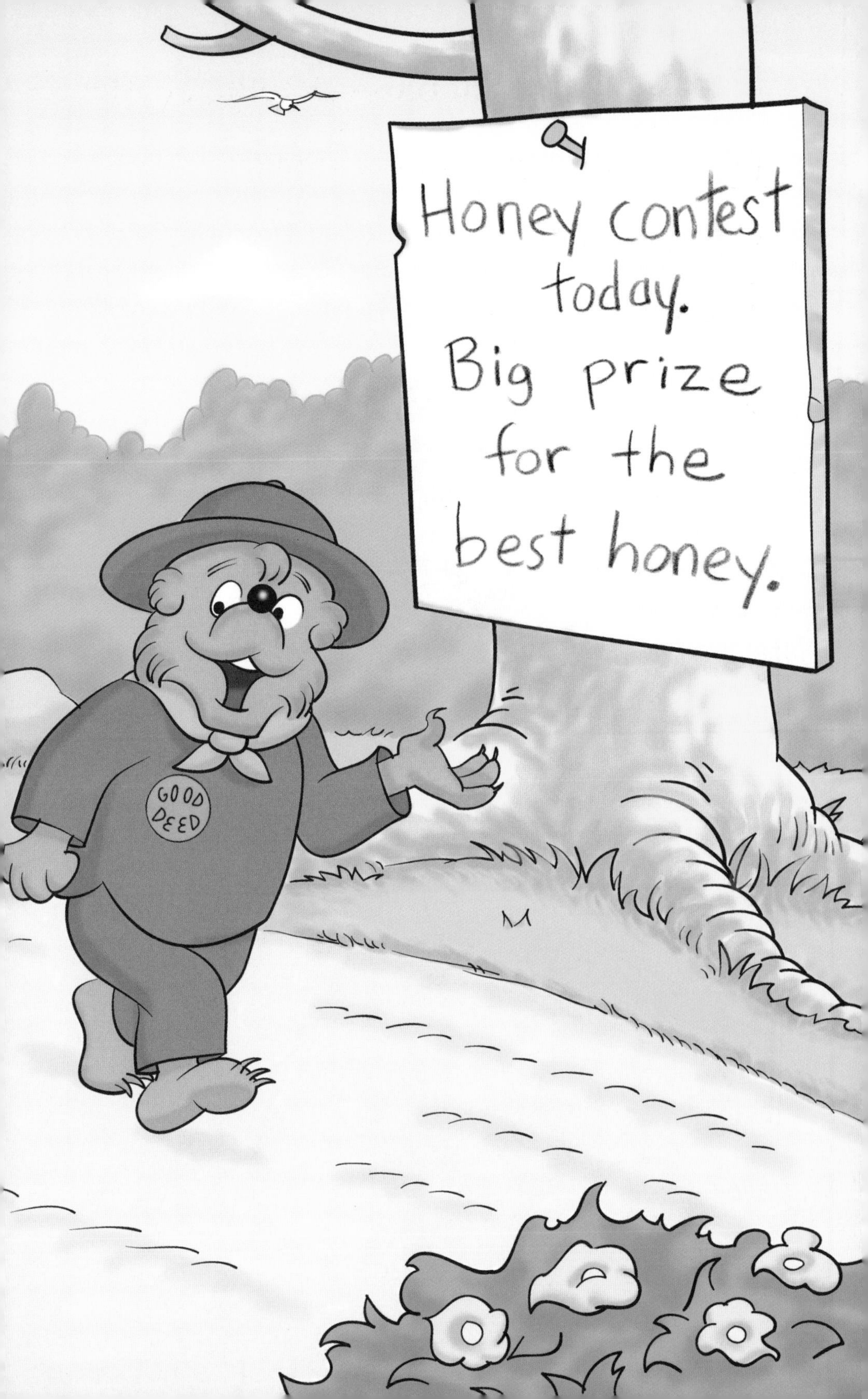
Honey contest today.
Big prize for the best honey.
GOOD DEED

Papa saw the sign too.

"I will win the prize

with my wild honey," said Papa.

"Where do you get wild honey, Papa?"

asked Sister.

"From the wild bee tree," said Papa.

"I am going on a honey hunt."

"We will help you, Papa," said Brother.

"That will be our good deed for the day."

"Thank you," said Papa to the scouts.

"I will show you how to hunt honey."

"As the Bible says," pointed out Fred,

"'A wise son brings joy to his father.'"

"Good point, Fred," said Brother.

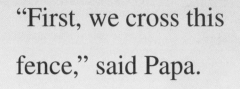

"First, we cross this fence," said Papa.

But Papa got caught.

"We will help," said the scouts.

"Thank you," said Papa.

"These fences are higher than they look."

"Now, we find a bee," said Papa.

"He will lead us to the wild bee tree."

Papa could not find a bee.

But a bee found him.

"YEOW!" Papa yelled.

"We will help,"

said the scouts.

"There goes the bee!"

"Thank you," said Papa.

"Bees are hard to find these days."

"Now, we cross this stream," said Papa.

But Papa slipped and fell in … SPLASH!!

"We will help," said the scouts.

"Thank you," said Papa.

"Stones are slipperier than they used to be."

Papa followed the bee across a field.

A bull lived in the field.

"It is hot today!" said Papa.

He took out a red cloth and waved it
in front of his face.

The bull saw the cloth and charged.

"We will help!" yelled Brother. "This way!"

"Thank you," said Papa.

"Bulls are faster than I remember."

Papa followed the bee

through a hollow log.

But he did not fit.

"We will help," said the scouts.

"Thank you," said Papa.
"I guess hollow logs are
smaller than before."

Papa followed the bee into Big Bear Bog.

But he sank right in.

"We will help," said the scouts. They got a rope and yanked Papa out.

"Thank you," said Papa. "That bog is boggier than I thought."

Papa followed the bee to the edge of a lake.

The bee flew across the lake.

"There he goes!" said Papa.

"We will help," said Sister.

"We will row you across."

"Thank you," said Papa.

"They made this lake wider, I think."

At last, the bee came to his honey tree.

Papa was happy.

"I can almost taste the wild honey!" Papa said.

"Look at all that honey!" said Papa.

But the bees were very angry.

"Look out!" called the scouts.

"Do not worry!" said Papa.

Papa picked the scouts up and ran.

He was faster than the bees.

He left them far behind.

"Look!" said Papa. "Farmer Ben

is winning the honey prize."

"Yum!" said the scouts. "We love honey."

"As the Bible says," pointed out Fred,

"'What is sweeter than honey?'"

"Good point, Fred," said Brother.

Ben gave them all a taste

of his special honey.

"Thanks for helping me, scouts," said Papa.

"You are welcome, Papa," said Brother.

"We like to help you," said Sister.

"As it says in the Bible," Fred pointed out,

"it is good to 'show respect for the elderly.'"

"Hmmm!" said Papa. "Good point, Fred—

I guess!"